For my dad, who inspired a fondness for nonsense and numbers

Acknowledgments

I am enormously grateful to mathemagician and educator extraordinaire Maggie Siena for her keen insight and guidance.

I am tremendously thankful to Susan Vanicky, Karen Hatt, Barbara Ensor, April Stevens, and my husband, David Cowan, all of whom kindly moved me over to the next tree when I was barking up the wrong one.

For their cheerful additions and subtractions, I thank Aidan, Olive, Elinor, and Charlie.

And I am exceedingly grateful to Anne Schwartz and Lee Wade, who have taught me the simple sum that three heads are better than one.

Published in the United States by Schwartz & Wade Books, an imprint of Random House Children's Books, a division of Random House, Inc., New York.

SCHWARTZ & WADE BOOKS and colophon are trademarks of Random House, Inc.

www.randomhouse.com/kids

Educators and librarians, for a variety of teaching tools, visit us at www.randomhouse.com/teachers

Library of Congress Cataloging-in-Publication Data
Fisher, Valorie.
How high can a dinosaur count? : and other math mysteries / Valorie Fisher.— 1st ed.
p. cm.
ISBN 0-375-83608-X (trade)
ISBN 0-375-93608-4 (lib. bdg.)
1. Arithmetic—Juvenile literature. 2. Counting—Juvenile literature. I. Title.
QA115.F57 2006
513—dc22
2005010851
MANUFACTURED IN CHINA
10 9 8 7 6 5 4 3 2 1
First Edition

A note for parents and educators:

Throughout this book, I have chosen to represent all numbers as numerals to help simplify the math for our youngest readers. At the end, you will find four additional questions about each illustration. There are certainly more questions that can be asked, and it may be fun to make up some of your own. Keep in mind that simply reminding some children of all the math skills they have, such as skip counting, estimating, adding, and subtracting, may be the only key they need to solve a problem.

Answers at the back of the book

How High Can a Dinosaur Count?

And other math mysteries

Valorie Fisher

s… ks · new york

Tristan and Troy are always talk-talk-talking on the telephone. 6 telephones just rang for Tristan, and 4 rang for Troy. How many telephones rang for the twins?

No one can balance vegetables like Bessie. Believe it or not, once she balanced a tower of 8 beets! But today, when she tries to balance 8 beets, 3 fall! How many beets does Bessie balance today?

juggling
onions

Ogden is an orderly man. His watering can is spic-and-span, and the paint is perfect on his picket fence. It takes Ogden 1 hour to clean 2 windows! How long will it take him to clean all 4 windows?

Farm Fresh Eggs
2¢ each

Trixie and Sadie like to sip tea in the tub. Today, Trixie drinks 7 cups of tea and Sadie drinks 4 cups. How many more cups of tea does Trixie drink than Sadie?

10
crunchy
cookies
15
bags
CELERY
tea
T.E.DOUGHERTY,
CHICAGO, ILL.

The heavenly hats at
Madame Millie's Millinery
are brimming with blossoms,
butterflies, and bows.
Heloise wants all of them, but
she has only 2 dimes, 2 nickels,
and 3 pennies to spend.
Can Heloise buy a hat?

52¢
31¢
49¢
37¢
27¢
33¢
71¢
Sale!
starts Saturday

Daphne dines on daisies. For dinner she usually eats 15, but today she eats 6 fewer than usual. How many daisies does Daphne eat for dinner?

BEASTLY BEAST
19 MILES
ODOROUS OGRE
16 MILES
WINSOME WITCH
26 MILES

Dexter's train is late! He is desperate for something to do while he waits. He begins to notice numbers and has soon spotted every odd number from 1 to 20. Can you find them, too?

PLATFORM 15
REFRESHMENTS
Donuts
7¢
13¢
hot chocolate
LIMONE
train ticket
11¢
CONEY ISLAND
train ticket
19¢
OAXACA
train ticket
5¢
WAIKIKI
train ticket
29¢
CREAM HILL LAKE
train ticket
17¢
BRICK LANE
train ticket
9¢

Ichabod's ice cream flavors are enticing. Liam selects scoops of licorice, lemon, and lime. Boaz buys scoops of banana, beet, and bubble gum. Tex takes scoops of toffee, tomato, and tangerine. Pierre picks scoops of pineapple, pickle, and peapod. How many scoops of ice cream does Ichabod serve Liam, Boaz, Tex, and Pierre?

Ichabod's Ice Cream
10¢
per scoop

Dixie's dad loves to blow up balloons. One morning, he blows up 12 balloons and takes them outside. He bumps into Bo and begs Bo to take 3 balloons for himself and 1 for his dog. He greets Greta and gives her 5. He hands 3 to Dixie before stepping back inside. How many balloons does Dixie's dad have left?

12
lemonade
3¢

Fiona's flapjack stack is higher than her sisters'. Fifi and Flo want flapjack stacks that are just as tall. How many more flapjacks must Felix flip so that the sisters' stacks are all the same size?

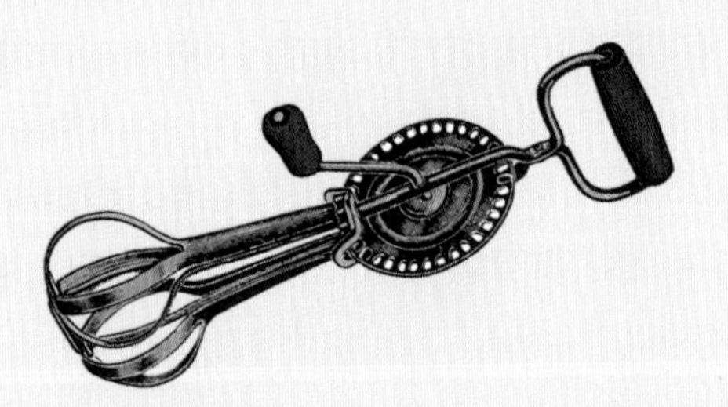

two trees
MAPLE SYRUP
2 Gallons
Two Frogs
BUTTERMILK
Pancake Mix
2 tons
2 lbs butter

Carmen's cakes are delicious. Bertram can't decide which flavors to choose for the layers of his birthday cake. He wants them all, except for mustard, lima bean, and potato! He can stack the layers on top of each other and make one towering treat. How many layers will Bertram's birthday cake have?

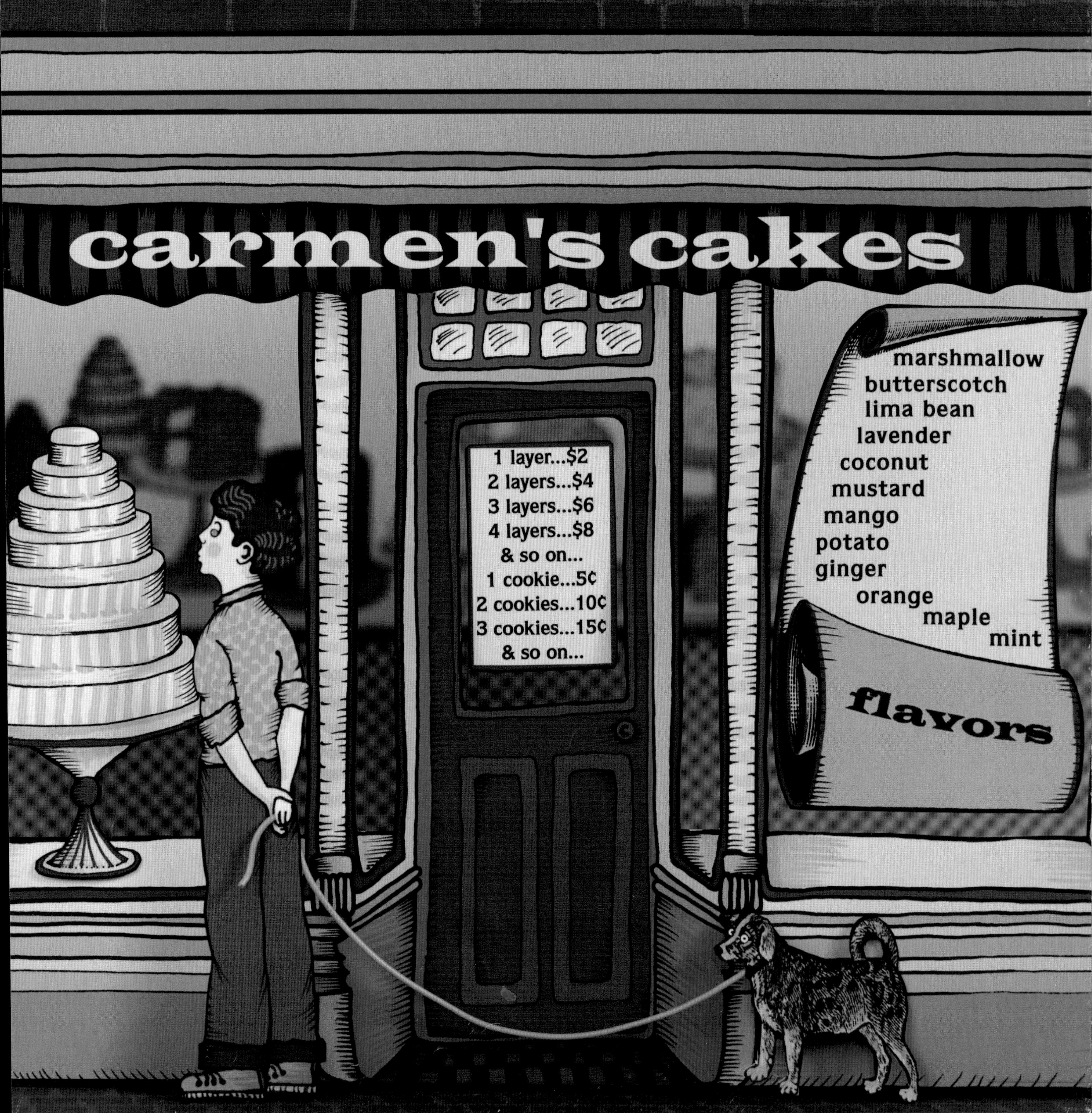
carmen's cakes
1 layer...$2
2 layers...$4
3 layers...$6
4 layers...$8
& so on...
1 cookie...5¢
2 cookies...10¢
3 cookies...15¢
& so on...
marshmallow
butterscotch
lima bean
lavender
coconut
mustard
mango
potato
ginger
orange
maple
mint
flavors

Fatima, the fortune-teller,

forecasts that Felicity will find

every even number from

0 to 20 in her booth.

Can you find them, too?

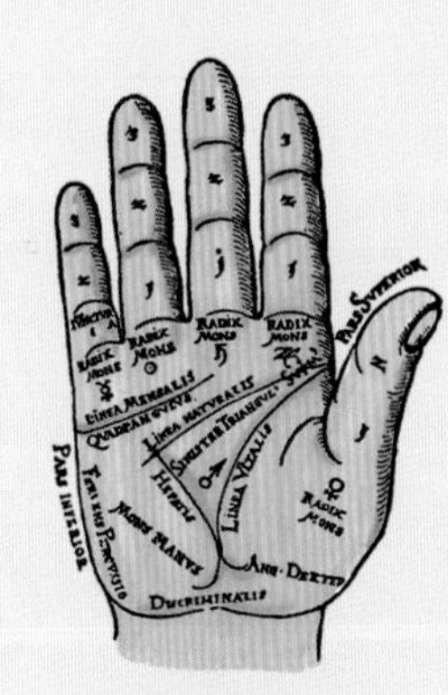

Fatima's
Fortune-Telling
open 4-8pm
tea leaves.... 20¢
tarot cards...0¢
crystal ball... $2
palm.... 10¢

Prunella pines for the pink polka-dotted purse in the window of Hattie's Handbags. Each of the purses she is holding contains 25¢. Does Prunella have enough to purchase the pink polka-dotted purse?

$1.30
75¢
99¢
$1.25
$1.00
98¢
$1.10
80¢
Hattie's Handbags

At the Loopy Laundromat, the washing machines slosh and spin but never wash a thing. Instead, they make fizzy fruit frappes. Each washing machine can make 5 frappes a day. How many frappes does the Loopy Laundromat make every day?

Loopy Laundromat
opens daily at
raspberry frappe 6¢
lemon-lime frappe 4¢
tangerine frappe 5¢
no spilling, no swilling
no slurping, no burping

Lulu loves to lick lollipops at
the Tutti-Frutti Zoo.
Unfortunately, today she has
come far too early. How long will
Lulu have to wait to
lick a luscious lollipop?

Tutti-Frutti Zoo
Lollipop Licking 3¢
Tangerine Taffy Tasting 5¢
Gooseberry Gumball Gobbling 2¢
Lollipop Licks
9 o'clock
seven days a week

More Math Mysteries to Solve!

Talk-Talk-Talking Twins

1. How many more telephones rang for Tristan than for Troy?
2. What numbers are missing from the small stack of blue books?
3. What numbers are missing from the small stack of green books?
4. What time is it?

Beet-Balancing Bessie

1. Can you find any groups of 3 in the picture?
2. Can you find any diamond shapes in the picture?
3. How many more beets does Bessie have than pumpkins?
4. Bessie can juggle an even number of onions that is less than 14 but more than 11. How many onions can she juggle?

Spic-and-Span Watering Can

1. Can you find any groups of 4 in the picture?
2. Can you find any rectangles in the picture?
3. How much would 4 eggs cost?
4. How many more pink flowers are there than purple flowers?

Tea in the Tub

1. How many cups of tea do they drink altogether?
2. Sadie likes pink and blue, but she doesn't like stripes. Can you tell which poodle is Sadie?
3. Each cup of tea used one tea bag. How many tea bags are left in the box?
4. If Trixie and Sadie share the box of cookies equally, how many cookies do they each get?

Madame Millie's Millinery

1. Which hat costs the least?
2. Which hat costs the most?
3. During the sale, all hats cost 7¢ less. What is the sale price of the beehive hat?
4. What is the sale price of the butterfly hat?

Dining on Daisies

1. At lunch, Daphne ate an odd number of daisies that is more than 5 but less than 9. How many daisies did Daphne eat at lunch?
2. At breakfast, Daphne ate 3 daisies. How many daisies did Daphne eat for the entire day—breakfast, lunch, and dinner?
3. Who lives the farthest away—the beast, the ogre, or the witch?
4. Who lives the closest?

A Knack for Noticing Numbers

1. How much does it cost to buy a cup of hot chocolate and a donut?
2. How much does it cost to buy a hot chocolate and a ticket to Limone?
3. How much more does it cost for a ticket to Waikiki than for one to Coney Island?
4. If you had 15¢, which train tickets could you buy?

Ichabod's Ice Cream

1. How much does Liam's ice cream cone cost?
2. Altogether, how much do the boys' ice cream cones cost?
3. Tex prefers that his scoops of tomato and tangerine ice cream do not touch. To keep Tex happy, how should his ice cream be stacked?
4. Pierre doesn't mind if his pineapple and peapod ice cream scoops touch, but his peapod scoop must not touch his pickle scoop. To keep Pierre happy, how should his ice cream be stacked?

Balloons

1. Can you find any ovals in the picture?
2. All the house numbers on Dixie's side of the street are even. What are the house numbers to the left and right of Dixie's house?
3. Dixie's dad bought lemonades for himself, Dixie, and Bo. He paid Greta with a dime. How much change did he get?
4. Greta sold 5 lemonades before she floated off. How much money did she make?

Flapjack Stacks

1. When all the stacks are the same size, how many flapjacks will Felix have made?
2. Can you find the number "2" and the word "two" in the picture?
3. Felix can eat an odd number of flapjacks that is more than 14 but less than 17. How many flapjacks can Felix eat?
4. Fifi and Flo both like stripes, but Fifi prefers long sleeves. Can you tell

which frog is Flo and which is Fifi?

Carmen's Cakes

1. How much will Bertram's birthday cake cost?
2. How much will the cake in the window cost?
3. How much will 5 cookies cost?
4. If you have 40¢ and buy 8 cookies, how much money will you have left?

Fortune-telling

1. Which fortune costs the most—tea leaves, tarot cards, crystal ball, or palm reading?
2. Which costs the least?
3. What number is missing from the stack of books?
4. What time is it?

Hattie's Handbags

1. Which handbag costs the most?
2. Which handbag costs the least?
3. If Prunella does not buy the pink polka-dotted purse, are there any other purses she can afford to buy?
4. If Prunella buys the green and orange plaid purse, how much change will she get?

The Loopy Laundromat

1. Can you find any circles in the picture?
2. What time does the Loopy Laundromat open?
3. How much will it cost to buy one frappe in each flavor?
4. 4 thirsty friends, with only 16¢, each want a frappe. Which flavor should they buy so that they each get a frappe?

Tutti-Frutti Zoo

1. Lulu wants to visit the Lollipop Licking 3 times. How much will it cost?
2. Lulu wants to visit the Tangerine Taffy Tasting 2 times and the Gooseberry Gumball Gobbling once. How much will it cost?
3. Lulu likes to lick lemon yellow lollipops, but not if they have blue swirls. Which lollipop might Lulu like to lick?
4. If you had 10¢ and wanted to spend it all at the Lollipop Licking and the Gooseberry Gumball Gobbling, how many times could you do each?

Solutions

Talk-Talk-Talking Twins
10 telephones rang for the twins.
1. 2. **2.** 7, 13, 17. **3.** 8, 11, 14, 16, 17. **4.** 3 o'clock.

Beet-Balancing Bessie
Bessie balances 5 beets today.
1. There are 3 buttons and 3 cabbages. **2.** There are diamonds on Bessie's dress and on her stand. **3.** 6. **4.** 12.

Spic-and-Span Watering Can
It will take Ogden 2 hours.
1. There are 4 windows, each with 4 panes; 4 small birds; 4 pink flowers; and 4 panels on the door. **2.** The door, the windows, and the sign are all rectangles. **3.** 8¢. **4.** 2.

Tea in the Tub
Trixie drinks 3 more cups of tea than Sadie.
1. 11. **2.** Sadie is on the right with a pink polka-dotted ribbon. **3.** 4. **4.** 5.

Madame Millie's Millinery
Heloise can buy one of 3 hats for 33¢, 31¢, or 27¢.
1. The pink striped hat for 27¢. **2.** The basket of flowers hat for 71¢. **3.** 42¢. **4.** 26¢.

Dining on Daisies
Daphne eats 9 daisies for dinner.
1. 7. **2.** 19. **3.** The witch. **4.** The ogre.

A Knack for Noticing Numbers
Dexter spotted odd numbers 1, 3, 5, 7, 9, 11, 13, 15, 17, and 19. Did you?
1. 20¢. **2.** 24¢. **3.** 10¢. **4.** Limone, Oaxaca, or Brick Lane.

Ichabod's Ice Cream
Ichabod serves the boys 12 scoops of ice cream.
1. 30¢. **2.** $1.20. **3.** Either tomato/toffee/tangerine or tangerine/toffee/tomato. **4.** Either pickle/pineapple/peapod or peapod/pineapple/pickle.

Balloons
Dixie's dad has 0 balloons left.
1. The balloons are ovals. **2.** 10 and 14. **3.** 1¢. **4.** 15¢.

Flapjack Stacks
Felix must flip 6 more flapjacks.
1. 18. **2.** On the pancake mix bag, the maple syrup container, and the butter. **3.** 15. **4.** Fifi is wearing a dress and Flo is wearing overalls.

Carmen's Cakes
Bertram's birthday cake will have 9 layers.
1. $18. **2.** $14. **3.** 25¢. **4.** 0¢.

Fortune-telling
Felicity found even numbers 0, 2, 4, 6, 8, 10, 12, 14, 16, 18, and 20. Did you?
1. Crystal ball. **2.** Tarot cards. **3.** 17. **4.** 6 o'clock.

Hattie's Handbags
Prunella can buy the pink polka-dotted purse with her $1.
1. The blue handbag for $1.30. **2.** The striped handbag for 75¢. **3.** Prunella can also afford to buy one of 4 handbags priced at 75¢, 80¢, 98¢, or 99¢. **4.** 20¢.

The Loopy Laundromat
The Loopy Laundromat makes 15 frappes a day.
1. The doors and the dials of the washing machines, the bubbles, and the clock are circles. **2.** 10 o'clock. **3.** 15¢. **4.** Lemon-lime.

Tutti-Frutti Zoo
Lulu will have to wait 1 hour.
1. 9¢. **2.** 12¢. **3.** The yellow lollipop with a red swirl. **4.** You could visit the Lollipop Licking and the Gooseberry Gumball Gobbling each 2 times, or you could visit the Lollipop Licking once and the Gooseberry Gumball Gobbling 3 times and have 1¢ left.